ABOUT THE BANK STREET READY-TO-READ SERIES

Seventy years of educational research and innovative teaching have given the Bank Street College of Education the reputation as America's most trusted name in early childhood education.

Because no two children are exactly alike in their development, we have designed the *Bank Street Ready-to-Read* series in three levels to accommodate the individual stages of reading readiness of children ages four through eight.

- *Level 1:* GETTING READY TO READ—read-alouds for children who are taking their first steps toward reading.
- *Level 2:* READING TOGETHER—for children who are just beginning to read by themselves but may need a little help.
- *Level 3:* I CAN READ IT MYSELF—for children who can read independently.

Our three levels make it easy to select the books most appropriate for a child's development and enable him or her to grow with the series step by step. The *Bank Street Ready-to-Read* books also overlap and reinforce each other, further encouraging the reading process.

We feel that making reading fun and enjoyable is the single most important thing that you can do to help children become good readers. And we hope you'll be a part of Bank Street's long tradition of learning through sharing.

The Bank Street College of Education

To my granddaughter,
Emily Sue. Welcome!
— J.O.

EENCY WEENCY SPIDER
A Bantam Little Rooster Book/November 1991

Little Rooster is a trademark of Bantam Books,
a division of Bantam Doubleday Dell Publishing Group, Inc.

Series graphic design by Alex Jay/Studio J
Editor: Gillian Bucky

Special thanks to James A. Levine, Betsy Gould,
Sally Doherty, and Cheryl Dixon.

Library of Congress Cataloging-in-Publication Data

Oppenheim, Joanne.
Eeency weency spider / by Joanne Oppenheim;
illustrated by S. D. Schindler.
p. cm. — (Bank Street ready-to-read)
"A Byron Preiss book."
"A Bantam little rooster book."
Summary: After climbing the water spout,
Eency Weency Spider meets Little Miss Muffet,
Humpty Dumpty, and Little Jackie Horner.
ISBN 0-553-07316-8. — ISBN 0-553-35304-7 (pbk.)
1. Nursery rhymes. 2. Children's poetry.
[1. Nursery rhymes.]
I. Schindler, S. D., ill. II. Title. III. Series.
PZ8.3.0615Ee 1991
811'.54—dc20
90-43572 CIP AC

Published simultaneously in the United States and Canada

PRINTED IN THE UNITED STATES OF AMERICA

0 9 8 7 6 5 4 3 2 1

Bank Street Ready-to-Read™

Eency Weency Spider

by Joanne Oppenheim
Illustrated by S. D. Schindler

A Byron Preiss Book

A BANTAM LITTLE ROOSTER BOOK
NEW YORK · TORONTO · LONDON · SYDNEY · AUCKLAND

The Eency Weency Spider
went up the water spout.

Down came the rain
and washed
the spider
out!

Out came the sun
and dried up all the rain.
And the Eency Weency Spider
went up the spout again.

Oh, Eency Weency Spider,
weave your silvery web.
Oh, Eency Weency Spider,
spin your silvery thread.
Upsy-downsy
outs and ins,
see how Eency Weency spins!

The Eeency Weency Spider
began to spin a bed.

Round and round
and up and down,
it spun its sticky thread.

Along came a fly
who stopped to take a nap.

"HA!" laughed the spider,
"I've caught you in my trap!"

Oh, Eency Weency Spider,
weave your silvery web.
Oh, Eency Weency Spider,
spin your silvery thread.
Upsy-downsy
outs and ins,
see how Eency Weency spins!

The Eency Weency Spider
was swinging to and fro.

When he heard a girl cry,
"Oh, no! No! No!"

Poor little Miss Muffet
had just come out to play.

But the Eency Weency Spider
frightened her away!

Oh, Eency Weency Spider,
weave your silvery web.
Oh, Eency Weency Spider,
spin your silvery thread.
Upsy-downsy
outs and ins,
see how Eency Weency spins!

The Eency Weency Spider
went climbing up a wall.

Step by step
it climbed and climbed—
that wall was ten feet tall.

There sat Humpty Dumpty
on the tippy top.
Till he saw the spider

and down he fell
          Kerplop!

Oh, Eency Weency Spider,
weave your silvery web.
Oh, Eency Weency Spider,
spin your silvery thread.
Upsy-downsy
outs and ins,
see how Eency Weency spins!

Little Jackie Horner
was eating cherry pie.
He pulled out a spider
and hollered, "My, oh my!"

The Eency Weency Spider
heard little Jackie cry.
But Eency Weency Spider
never blinked an eye!

The Eency Weency Spider
scurried out of sight.
But poor little Jack
had quite an awful fright.

That's why Jack was nimble.
That's why Jack was quick.
When he saw the spider,
he jumped the candlestick!

Oh, Eency Weency Spider,
weave your silvery web.
Oh, Eency Weency Spider,
spin your silvery thread.
Upsy-downsy
outs and ins,
see how Eency Weency spins!